Weekly Reader Children's Book Club presents

The Chimp That Went To School

(Original title: Mr. Adams's Mistake)

By Peggy Parish
Pictures by Gail Owens

Macmillan Publishing Co., Inc.
New York
Collier Macmillan Publishers
London

For Bubba Davis, with love

This book is a presentation of
Weekly Reader Children's Book Club.

Weekly Reader Children's Book Club
offers book clubs for children from
preschool through junior high school.
For further information write to:
Weekly Reader Children's Book Club
1250 Fairwood Ave.
Columbus, Ohio 43216

Macmillan Publishing Co., Inc.
866 Third Avenue, New York, N.Y. 10022
Collier Macmillan Canada, Inc.
Printed in the United States of America

10 9 8 7 6 5 4 3 2 1

Library of Congress
Cataloging in Publication Data
Parish, Peggy.
Mr. Adams's mistake.

(Ready-to-read)
Summary: Mistaking him for a
child, a near-sighted truant officer
takes a chimpanzee to school.
[1. School stories. 2. Chimpanzees—
Fiction. 3. Humorous stories]
I. Owens, Gail, ill. II. Title.
III. Title: Mister Adams's mistake. IV. Series.
PZ7.P219Mr [E] 81-17221
ISBN 0-02-769800-9 AACR2

This edition is published by arrange-
ment with Macmillan Publishing
Company.

Mr. Adams had a special job.
"Children must go to school,"
he said.
"They have a lot to learn.
And they learn in school."

Mr. Adams walked
along the street.
"Some children try
to skip school," he said.
"I must find those children.
I must take them to school.
That is my special job."

Mr. Adams worked hard.

But he did not see well.

And he would not get eyeglasses.

So he made mistakes.

Sometimes he took

the wrong things to school.

One day he took
a dancing poodle.

One day he took
a big doll.

One day he tried to take

his grandmother.

But she bopped him hard.

Mr. Adams came to the corner.

He stopped to buy

a newspaper from Dan.

Corky was Dan's helper.

Mr. Adams looked at Corky.

"How old is he?" asked Mr. Adams.

"Corky is seven," said Dan.

"He should be in school,"

said Mr. Adams.

"But he is a chimpanzee!"

said Dan.

"Nonsense," said Mr. Adams.

"A chimpanzee does not wear a

red sweater."

He took Corky's hand.

"Come along," he said.

And Corky went.

"Don't worry, Corky,"

called Dan.

"I will get you back."

But Corky was not worried.

Children went to school.

Corky loved children.

He wanted to go to school, too.

Soon Corky and Mr. Adams
came to the schoolhouse.
Corky was so excited
he began to chatter.
"Hush up," said Mr. Adams.
"You must be quiet in school."

They went inside.

"Let me see," said Mr. Adams.

"Yes, here is your room."

He opened the door.

"Miss Nelson," said Mr. Adams,

"here is a new boy.

His name is Corky."

"Boy?" said Miss Nelson.

"He looks like a chimpanzee."

"Shh," said Mr. Adams.

"He can't help

the way he looks."

Mr. Adams left quickly.
"Oh, my goodness,"
said Miss Nelson.

"Class, this is Corky.
He will be with us today."
She took Corky's hand.
"You sit here," she said.

"He really is a chimpanzee,"
said Jack.

"I know," said Miss Nelson.

"But Mr. Adams thinks he is a boy.
We will just have to make
the best of it."

The children all laughed.

"Mr. Adams does get mixed up,"
said Sara.
"Well, never mind,"
said Miss Nelson.
"It is time for reading."
The children opened
their reading books.
"This story will tell you
all about peanuts,"
said Miss Nelson.
Corky liked peanuts.
He began to chatter.
"All right, Corky,"
said Miss Nelson.
"Here is a book for you."

Corky looked at the book.

He saw pictures of peanuts.

He really wanted to hear
the story.

Corky listened hard,
but he did not hear a thing.

He shook the book.

He put it on his head.

He put it on the floor.

He jumped on it.

But the book would not
tell him about peanuts.

Corky got mad.

He picked up the book.
He started to throw it.

"No! No, Corky!"
said Miss Nelson.
She took the book.

"All right, class,"
said Miss Nelson.
"Let's have art."
"Come on, Corky,"
said Nancy.
"I will get you some clay.
You will like that."
Nancy got the clay.
She put it on the table.
Corky looked at the clay.
He patted it.
He punched it.
Corky liked the way
the clay felt.

Corky tasted the clay.

YUCK!

Corky did not like
the way it tasted.

He did not like it one bit.

Corky picked up the clay.

He rolled it in his hands.

He looked at it.

He had made a ball!

Corky knew about balls.
Balls were to throw,
so Corky threw his ball.

Oops! Over went the fish bowl.

CRASH! The bowl broke.

The fish flip-flopped
on the floor.

"Our fish!" said Amy.

"They will die without water."

Corky scooped up the fish.
He dumped them
in the turtle's bowl.
"Oh, no!" said Robert.
"The turtle will eat the fish."

Corky scooped up the turtle.
He dumped it
in the bird's water bowl.
"Oh, no!" said Sally.
"The bird will peck the turtle."

Corky scooped up the bird.

He looked all around.

There was no place
to put the bird.

Corky ran to the window.

"No! No!" shouted the children.

Annie ran to Corky.

She took the bird from him.

Miss Nelson found another bowl
for the fish.
Soon all was right again.

"Maybe Corky should paint,"
 said Betsy.
"I will get some paper."
"Here, Corky," said Nancy.
"Here is a paint brush.
 Here is some red paint."
"Red," said Miss Nelson.
"Your sweater is red, Corky."

"I wish I had a red sweater,"
said Jim.

Corky looked at the paint.

He looked at Jim's sweater.

And he painted it red.

"No! No!" said Miss Nelson.

"Paint on the paper."

But Corky did not listen.
He was having fun.
Corky painted stripes
on Janie.

He painted Al's hair.

He painted Mary's shoes.
He tried to paint
Miss Nelson's face.
"Stop it! Stop it!"
shouted the children.

"You are bad!"

shouted Mary.

Corky did not like shouting.

He did not like it one bit.

He looked at the children.

They looked angry.

They looked very angry.

Corky was scared.
What should he do?
He looked at the
angry children again.

And Corky ran.

The children ran after him.

They shouted at him.

Corky saw the bookshelves.

He began to climb.

Up, up, climbed Corky.

He climbed to the top shelf.

He got in a corner,

and he hid his face.

The children looked at him.

"I think he is crying,"

said Jack.

"Poor Corky," said Mary.

"He looks so sad."

"Oh, Corky," said Jim.

"We are sorry we shouted.

Please come down.

We won't hurt you."

Corky peeked at the children.

They smiled at him.

Corky was not scared now.

He started to climb down.

Suddenly the door opened.

Dan ran in.

A policeman ran in.

Mr. Adams ran in.

He was very angry.

"Show me a chimpanzee!"

he shouted.

"If there is one in this class,

my face is red!"

Corky dropped his paint.

SPLASH!

Mr. Adams was red all over.

Corky jumped into Dan's arms.
"There is the chimpanzee!"
shouted the children.

Mr. Adams did not say a word.

He started to leave.

"Where are you going?"
asked the policeman.

"To get some eyeglasses,"
said Mr. Adams.

"I guess I do need them."

"No! No!" shouted the children.

"Then you won't bring
fun things to school.
You won't bring Corky again.
And we love him."

Mr. Adams went out.

But he soon came back

with ice cream for everyone.

Mr. Adams did get eyeglasses.
But he still brought Corky
to visit the children.
That made everyone happy.